The Mother of St.

A Story of Duty and Peril

Grant Balfour

Alpha Editions

This edition published in 2023

ISBN : 9789357932806

Design and Setting By
Alpha Editions
www.alphaedis.com
Email - info@alphaedis.com

Contents

CHAPTER I.

WATCHING FOR THE PREY.

Go back into the third century after Christ, travel east into the famous Mediterranean Sea, survey the beautiful south-west coast of Asia Minor, and let your eyes rest on the city of Patara. Look at it well. Full of life then, dead and desolate now, the city has wonderful associations in sacred and legendary lore—it saw the great reformer of the Gentiles, and gave birth to the white-haired man of Christmas joy.

Persecution had beforetime visited Patara, in common with other parts of the Roman Empire; and there were ominous signs, like the first mutterings of an earthquake, that a similar calamity might come again. The prejudice and malice of the common people were dangerously stirred up to fight the quiet, persistent inroads of aggressive Christianity.

The authorities, perplexed and exasperated, were disposed to wink at assault upon individual Christians, to try them on any plausible pretext, and to shew them little quarter. If they could arrest the ringleaders, especially people of rank or wealth, whether men or women, in anything wrong or strongly suspicious, that they might apply exemplary punishment, then the irritated majority might be satisfied, and peace in the city restored.

In a recess at the corner of a busy street, leading towards the market place, two men stood, waiting and watching for some particular person to pass by. They were Demonicus and Timon, whose office or duty was something like that of a modern detective.

Demonicus, clad in a brown *chiton* or tunic reaching down to the knees, was a powerfully built, dark man, with great bison-like shoulders and thick neck, bristling eyebrows, and fierce, covetous eyes. To him nothing was too perilous or too mean where there was strife or the chance of gold. He was a wrestler and mighty swordsman, he had often fought in the stadium or circus, and his fame had travelled as far as Rome, to which he went at last, and greatly distinguished himself for a time.

Timon, similarly clad, was only a man of ordinary strength; but he was lithe, self-willed and shrewd, with a streak of courtesy and sympathy.

Camels, bullocks, horses, mules and wagons were passing by—a picturesque train of noisy, dusty movement on an unpaved street—while now and again a carriage or a litter appeared, whose occupants were considered either arrogant, or effeminate.

"Her carriage must have passed," said Demonicus savagely.

"It cannot be," replied Timon civilly; "the lady, though unfettered by custom, rarely takes her carriage; she usually passes on foot shortly after the morning meal, and I came here to watch in ample time."

"We must arrest her to-day on some pretext or other," muttered Demonicus. "I shall dog her steps everywhere, and if I cannot get a good excuse I shall invent one. The bribe," added he with an impatient gesture, "is too tempting for more delay."

Timon, though also grasping, was not heart and soul with Demonicus. When on the watch alone he had had time to reflect, and his better nature would now and again assert itself, as there stole over his vision a beautiful figure with a noble work in hand. He wanted the prize but was not in hot haste to win it, and while it seemed judicious it also felt agreeable to suggest delay. After a brief silence he remarked—

"There is to be a special gathering of the Christians in the Church of the Triple Arch to-night. The bishop is away at Myra. But Orestes, the shepherd, is to be present, and I promise thee something will be said that will give us a plausible backing; his words are plain, ay even bold as the cliffs of Mount Taurus, where he dwells. Should we not wait till then, Demonicus?"

"I shall not," answered he, stamping his heavy, sandalled foot viciously; "it would be our last chance, and the woman might not be there."

"The lady is sure to be," rejoined Timon, "she is the spirit of the whole movement."

Demonicus paced about reflecting, and having cooled down, he mumbled,— "I shall see, but I shall miss no chance before."

Timon now stepped out and looked along the street, then turning immediately round to his companion with a hesitating, half-regretful look, he whispered—

"She is coming!"

The face of Demonicus glowed with an evil flame, as he went forward quickly to assure himself. The lady with her attendant, a liberated female slave, was seen approaching on foot, and both men retreated into the recess and waited.

CHAPTER II.

A MINISTERING ANGEL.

Pathema, the eldest daughter of a prosperous merchant, walked with her servant Miriam through the crowded street, heedless or unconscious of danger; then passing two pairs of eyes directed towards her veiled face, she turned at right angles into the Stenos, a short quiet street leading towards the river Xanthus.

Without haste, yet her progress was steady and good, with a natural grace set free by the loose Ionic dress—a cream-coloured *chiton*, girdled at the waist and falling from the shoulders to the feet in many folds, and above it a short mantle in gold-brown, bordered with white. Full of work of a high order, her dark eyes and finely carved mouth spoke beneficent purpose, while her fair countenance showed an Oriental seriousness and thought.

Pathema might have spared herself a life of labour and risk and self-sacrifice. She might have enjoyed a life of fashion and pleasure and ease. Besides this, her beauty and accomplishments could have easily secured for her a home and affluence, had she so desired. But she had cast in her lot with One who had lived a higher life, which in working-out had made him a man of "no reputation." Pathema was a Christian, and as such had made herself a set of determined and malicious enemies. Her Christianity could not be mistaken. There was no mere form about it, no casual acts of duty, no hysterical nights, no insipidity, and no compromise,—the gods must go. It was a clear, steady, every-day light, peeping up in childhood, and burning brighter and brighter thro' the years. Though a lover of knowledge and fond of reasoning, she wasted no time in a vain jangle about faith and works, but illustrated both in her daily life. Encouraged by her parents, and acting as their medium, and that of other benefactors, she attended to the wants of a wide circle of sick and poor, both heathen and Christian. Like her Lord himself, she went about doing good. No one cheered and comforted the members of the Christian community more, no one was a greater inspiration, and no one was more unassuming.

On the left bank of the Xanthus stood a large residence belonging to a man of wealth, a business friend of Pathema's father. In front there was no altar to Apollo Agyieus, and no statue of any god, the owner having distinct leanings toward Christianity. All that met the eye was a Victor's Laurel tree, behind the house, which was much greater in depth than width, was a garden, containing such trees as pomegranate, orange, and fig.

To that house Pathema went. Ascending the steps and knocking at the door, she was met by a porter (with his dog), who led her and Miriam past his lodge and along the narrow passage to the first peristyle—a partly open courtyard. Here they awaited the appearance of the mistress. On all four sides were colonnades, under which were a banqueting room, a picture gallery, a library, servants' office, sitting rooms, and several bed-chambers. The visitors had not long to wait.

"Peace be with you!" said the mistress, with a gracious smile.

"Joy to thee!" was the reply.

Entering a chamber on the right, Pathema was gently conducted to the bedside of Crito, an invalid boy, his parents' pride and tender care. Crito had received a good education, and, when well, was active, witty and intelligent. But he had been hurt internally while wrestling in the gymnasium with an older lad, and for a time his life hung in the balance. Several days had elapsed since Pathema saw him, and he was now fast asleep. She did not speak, but looked on him awhile with earnest anxious eyes. At length a gleam of hope lit up her face, and she was about to leave softly when Crito, as if conscious of some departing force, suddenly opened his eyes.

"Hail! Pathema; steal not thyself away," said he smiling.

"I steal but a gem of hope—surely a lighter load," was the laughing answer.

"And yet thou hast left it in my breast, thou absent-minded robber."

Bending down, Pathema kissed his bosom, saying, "And I am glad to leave it there."

"And go forth hopeless?" queried he.

"Yes," said she, shaking her head in feigned solemnity, and Crito laughed.

Leaving figures of speech, Pathema expressed her joy that there appeared to be good ground for hope. Then they entered into an animated conversation about the Iliad and the Odyssey, books that the Hellenic people used as we do Robinson Crusoe, Shakespeare, and the Bible. Before parting they conversed about the Memoirs of the Apostles, called in our day the Gospels.

"I love the Nazarene's moral courage," said Crito.

"Yes," replied Pathema, "to be invited, for instance, to dine with a number of the learned, and without personal provocation to feel compelled to denounce them as hypocrites, must have been a severe trial of his courage."

"It seems easier to face wounds and the loss of blood than the loss of reputation," rejoined Crito.

"It is, but, of course, the full test is to face both. The applause of his comrades, of the whole army and of his nation, fires the spirit of the brave soldier that climbs the frowning walls of a besieged city; but the Nazarene had not the applause of a single soul when He faced the certainty of cruel death upon the cross; worse, there was derision, and He himself even cried out that God had forsaken Him."

"The cross means a great deal," said Crito reflectively.

"It was endured in love for us," was the reply.

"The love was great," remarked the boy.

Pathema now rose up to go, and Crito was very sorry; but he knew that there were many other poor and tried ones waiting to welcome her, and he urged himself to resignation.

"Come back on the morrow," said he, "and stay with me longer; I weary much for thee."

Having kissed her hand respectfully, the boy looked after her wistfully as she departed like a heavenly angel.

Going next into the humble abode of an old man, whose only attendant was a little granddaughter, Pathema with her maid proceeded at once to put the place in thorough order, aiding the slender one with the heaviest work, such as it was. The child had always done well, but stronger arms could of course do better, and everything was soon in special dress. Then Pathema had a comforting talk with the grandfather and with his faithful little servant-maid, ending by telling her a charming tale of a Forest Nymph. Before leaving she placed a silver coin in the old man's trembling hand; and as she departed, he could only say, "God bless thee," while the child clung to her sympathetic hand for some distance along the street.

Thus Pathema, accompanied by her servant, went from house to house a messenger of mercy. The harvest-field of suffering and privation was then, as ever, white; but the reapers were few, and of modern reaping instruments—hospitals and "homes"—there were none. How much Christianity has done, yet how much to do!

Partaking of a plain mid-day meal of *maza*, barley bread, and figs, with a venerable heathen widow whose heart was opening to Christianity, she also supplied this poor one's need, and resumed her journey refreshed.

The afternoon was well advanced when they passed underneath the Triple Arch of the city wall on their way outward to a sheltered spot not far beyond. In a clump of olive trees and beside a limpid spring, they came upon a hut occupied by motherless children, alone and unprotected, the hireling having left the day before. Sadder still, the only one old enough to give material help, and who did help as long as she was able, Biona, a girl of twelve, was dying of consumption. The sight to Pathema was very distressing, but she attended promptly to the wants of the sick one, laving her face and hands, and giving her a little nourishment, while Miriam looked after the younger children and the house.

Biona was somewhat revived, and Pathema sat down beside her to whisper just a consoling word or two at intervals. The girl expressed heir gratitude briefly, showing it more in her large, hollow but brilliant eyes, which rested for a time in peace on her visitor's tender face. The peace was of short duration, for Biona was very feeble. She moved her head and hands uneasily in the hot air of the little room, and at last exclaimed in a low plaintive voice—"Oh! for breath and rest, rest."

"Let me carry thee out, my dear, as thy father does, and lay thee among the olive trees," said Pathema, feeling keenly, while she held the invalid's thin, white hand bearing the marks of toil.

"Thou art not able," replied Biona huskily, and with grateful tears, adding to herself in a dreamy whisper—"My father, poor father!"

But Pathema was wiry and enduring, easily fit for the fragile burden, and having by a word persuaded the sufferer she wrapped her in a long white *chiton*, and carried her with great tenderness out into the cooler welcome air, beside the refreshing spring.

"How delightful is rest!" said the dying girl, as she gazed up through the olive branches into the clear blue sky.

"There is abundance of rest in store, my beloved, even the rest that remaineth for the people of God."

Biona lay quietly, enjoying a measure of peace. Her pet white dove, flying from an overhanging branch, came down beside her; it hopped upon the pillow, and with gentle wing softly brushed her pallid cheek. She turned her head toward it, and gazing fondly upon the affectionate creature, forgot her weariness for a time—a little time. Then she began to move her head restlessly, whispering often and with yearning look the word father.

The watchful attendant changed the weary one's position, and gave her rest again. This was done as often as it was needed, and the need had no end. Pathema prayed earnestly for the sufferer's recovery or release. Her voice was the heart's melody, soft and soothing, if to soothe were possible.

The father, a big sympathetic man, had by this time reached the bordering olive trees, on his way home from a brief search for aid. His clothing was very simple and plain: a dark *exomis* (a short sleeveless frock), and shoes of leather, studded with nails. As was common, he was bareheaded. He had a melancholy foreboding that calamity was near at hand. His oxen stood idle in their stall from early morning. Noticing with surprised relief that his child was already out in the grove, with some merciful one reclining by her side, he stole up a little nearer and halted unobserved.

"Oh! for rest, rest," his daughter faintly cried; and the strong man shook with emotion. "Oh! that I might be at rest!" she cried again, as if a last feeble effort, "but how hard it is, how hard! to leave my little brothers and my poor lonely father."

Creeping closer, Pathema raised Biona's weary head and placed it tenderly in her own bosom. Feeling that the spark of life was low (for the little hands were getting cold), and that words were unavailing, she closed her eyes and became absorbed in silent prayer.

A little interval and then, with pleading face, the simple words of the child—

"Father in heaven, take into thy kind care my father and brothers;"

And then, with a peaceful smile—

"Oh mother, I come!"

The father came forward delicately and softly behind and looked down, his eyes full of tears. The child raised her languid eyes and smiled, a strange, yearning heavenly smile; then she drew a deep breath and fell asleep—her rest, the long last rest, had come.

Let the veil lie drawn tenderly over the poor father's sorrow. It is sufficient to say that everything was done for his beloved one and his home that could be done before Pathema and her faithful servant left. The mourner's gratitude, deep and full, was their comfort and reward.

"My mistress," said Miriam, in an entreating respectful voice as they turned towards the city in weary sad silence, "thou art much in need of rest; wilt thou not proceed home, for the gathering of our people will be well-nigh broken up ere we pass by?" Miriam was wise and good, she loved her mistress fervently, and was trusted and treated as a companion, not as a liberated slave.

"We pass the door, my Miriam, and it would be a rest to turn aside and listen to the life-giving Word," answered Pathema, looking tenderly into the devoted woman's tired face; "yet for thy sake, thy needful release, I shall go on with thee."

"No, my mistress, no,—thy desire is good and right."

The Church of the Triple Arch was not far away, and the two plodded patiently and trustfully back into the city, thinking not of any danger that might come. Their day's work was done—hard and heart-trying, yet beautiful, and as an exercise of mercy, beneficial to subject as well as object, for "there is that scattereth and yet increaseth." Good were it for the world if all mankind did their possible and necessary share. The moon shone high and clear in the star-lit temple of the sky. The night was calm, and nothing broke the stillness save the discordant, mocking cry of a laughing hyena far behind, with an occasional, distant shout rising from the city in front. As they emerged from the olive-grove, the pet white dove, pursued by a swift-winged night-hawk, swept like an arrow across their track, as if an omen of coming trouble.

CHAPTER III

STILL ON THE WATCH.

Demonicus and Timon stood at the open door of the Christian church, not far from the Triple Arch of the city wall, listening to the voice of the shepherd Orestes, and eagerly watching for something whereby they might seize him and certain others. But Demonicus, *sycophantes*, constable, and gladiator all in one, was irritated, for the prize had not yet arrived; and as the time sped on, his tiger-nature exhibited itself in low growls at his calmer companion.

"Another day," snarled he, "and the case will have turned into other hands."

"I do not despair," replied Timon, "and yet, to be frank, I almost repent—it seems a shame to lay hands on such a woman."

"Art thou, my brave Timon, also becoming a meek and beautiful Christian?" said Demonicus with a sneer.

Annoyed at the tone, Timon answered firmly—"The lady's life is a blessing to Patara."

"Soft one, weak one, coward!" hissed Demonicus.

"The lady is a goddess!" cried Timon, galled into defiance, "and the coward is he that would lay foul hands upon her."

"Draw! defend thyself!" roared Demonicus, and the two men faced each other with drawn swords and glaring eyes.

At this juncture, Pathema and Miriam appeared upon the scene, and without hesitation the former gently and earnestly entreated them not to slay one another. As if by mutual consent, the enraged men lowered their sword-points and turned them into the sheaths. Demonicus was agreeably surprised and he cooled down quickly—before him after all was the trophy wanted. Timon did not want it—the lady's voice and courage strengthened his heart's bent in the right course, and he quietly walked away. Demonicus stepped aside; even his rough heart could be moved to a certain degree of respect, while Pathema, pale and sad, walked noiselessly into the church and sat down with Miriam in the nearest empty seat.

The shepherd had finished with his earnest simple story of redemption, illustrating it by reference to what he knew so well—the spotless, passive lamb. He was now telling the attentive listeners that the lamb would one clay become a lion, that all human governments would be broken in pieces, and that Jesus Christ would rule the earth in righteousness and peace. "It may be," added he with emphasis, "that that hope-inspiring day is at hand!"

Revolutionary doctrine like this the debased Demonicus rejoiced to hear. Like the Jewish pretence before Pilate, it was enough, and the love of lucre spurred him on. He waited not a moment more, but hurried boldly into the church. Accusing Pathema of taking part in sedition, he seized her by the arm and ordered her to rise up and follow him.

Startled at this interruption, the people looked round, while Orestes stopped and made his way swiftly to Pathema's aid, thinking in all simplicity that a robber or a madman had entered the church. The gladiator was strong, but the shepherd was stronger, and ere the former could draw his sword he was pinned to the floor as with an oaken hand. The spectacle was like the grappling of prostrate giants.

"Thou art guilty of sedition and violence!" yelled Demonicus.

Others of his official order passing by and hearing the noise, came quickly to his aid, the accusation was repeated, and the shepherd meekly submitted— he never meant to defy the law.

Miriam pleaded for her beloved mistress in tears, but she was rudely thrust aside as too insignificant for arrest.

Then were Pathema and Orestes and others led out of the church and into the street. They formed a silent, little company, surrounded and followed by an excited jeering crowd. And as the crowd increased in strength—"Death to the detested Christians!" was the noisy frequent cry.

With bowed head and weary heart, and with her sense of modesty painfully shocked, Pathema passed on with her fellow-Christians to the humiliating place of safe-keeping for the night.

Their trial came off next day, but it was a mockery. Fanatical hate and bribery did their foul work—there was no justice whatever, and sentence of death was passed!

An appeal was made to Rome.

To that great city Pathema and her fellow prisoners were finally transported, and there they were imprisoned.

Among the poor and sick and dying of Patara and its neighbourhood, was no one more missed and mourned than the compassionate maiden who languished and wept in a far away Roman prison—wept, not so much for her own wrongs, as for the griefs and pains of others.

"O Lord, I cry to Thee—
Unending night, a mournful robe,

Enwraps my form, and veils my sight
From flower, and stream, and all I love—
My bondage break, O God!

"If I no more behold
My Crito, Lord, on him look down
With watchful eye, and send Thy light,
Restore his strength, and make him Thine;
Regard my love for him.

"Biona's tender care
Provide for, Lord, and guard from ill;
The father's wound, in pity heal.
Remember all the desolate
For whom I weep and pray.

"My parents, Lord, uphold;
Their grief assuage; Thy Spirit send
And teach of Him who suffered more
Than mortal man, to ransom me
From death—the Christ, my strength.

"Yet, Lord, how hard to die
So soon. Oh! to behold the sun,
To breathe the air, to clasp the flowers,
Embrace my 'loved, now loved tenfold;
But, Lord, Thy will be done!"

CHAPTER IV.

THE AMPHITHEATRE.

The Colosseum or amphitheatre in Rome was a gigantic, costly building, oval in shape, 100 feet in height, 1900 feet in circumference, and capable of seating 100,000 spectators—a huge egg laid by Imperial power and demoniac love of pleasure. Its external wall rose up in three rows of columns, Doric, Ionic and Corinthian, forming 80 arcades or arches in each row, and was capped by a solid wall with Corinthian pilasters and small square windows. There was no roof, shelter from sun or rain being given by a movable awning called the *velarium*. The higher arcades were adorned with statues and chariots, and admitted light and air. Four of the basement arches at the extremities were the entrances for the great, while the remaining seventy-six were for the common people. Rising from the top of a low wall or balcony that stood on the ground many feet inward, was the *gradus* or slope of seats, which extended half-way up the high surrounding shell. The highest seats were a colonnade or portico reserved for women. On the slope under the portico, were the three *maeniana* or galleries, separated by walls and by landing places for the many staircases. The uppermost gallery, with benches of wood, was for the *pullati* or common people; the next below, for the *popularia*; and the farthest down, of stone or marble and cushioned, for members of the equestrian order. Below this was the inner wall or balcony (referred to above), called the *podium*, the place of honour, on which sat the Emperor and his family, senators, chief magistrates, vestal virgins, and distinguished visitors. The Emperor occupied a pavilion, named the *suggestus*, while the others sat on cushioned chairs or reclined on couches. The *podium* was about 15 feet from the ground, its edge bordered with metal trellis work, and its front faced with marble, to prevent the ascent of wild beasts when frightened or enraged. The arena was the immense space within, being about 281 feet by 176, and it was covered with sand, to keep the combatants from slipping and to absorb their blood. Here some of the martyrs of Jesus poured out their life, to gratify horrible curiosity, and to satiate the hunger of lions.

On a certain day in the latter half of the third century after Christ, and while the pagan Roman empire still held powerful sway, many thousands of people had assembled in the amphitheatre to witness a series of blood-curdling sights and combats. Among these sad spectacles was the suffering of a noted Christian from the rugged province of Lycia.

Demonicus, the great gladiator of Patara city, had fallen, his left cheek was embedded in the sand, his brawny upper arm lay out limp beside his broken sword, and his life-blood was streaming away. He would indulge in the love of strife and watch the footsteps of the innocent for glittering gold no more.

His conqueror, Telassar, a big bearded warrior from Rhaetia, stood erect and proud, with his right foot on the gladiator's neck, and drinking in the applause that flowed from the encircling host of sensation-loving, heartless spectators.

After a fierce and prolonged battle, several other gladiators had ploughed the sand in strange quick succession. Here, face downward, was a Samnite with his oblong shield; yonder lay a bare headed *retiarius* with his net and three-pointed lance. Twenty feet from Demonicus, a horseman clad in cuirass and helmet was stretched upon his back wounded and dying, with his round shield and lance lying near. His handsome black charger had instantly wheeled round, and it now stood over him with lowered neck in beautiful faithfulness, a tribute to its master's care and kindness. The other combatants were being hooked and drawn away like logs into the *spoliarium*, the grim receptacle for slaughtered men; the expiring horseman's turn would soon come. His rival had also reeled and tumbled down, the result of exhaustion from a severe wound received earlier in the fray. Aided by an official called a *lanista*, the victor's struggles to rise up and, when risen, to keep on his feet, were pitiable in the extreme. Deprived of its rider, his spirited grey horse, itself slightly wounded, was bounding round the arena like a frightened antelope. And considering that there was a circumference of 900 feet in which to galop and wheel, it gave its pursuers no small degree of trouble.

This state of affairs, coupled with the usual breathing time before the next act in the tragic drama, allowed the horde of onlookers an opportunity for a little conversation and even merriment. In the presence of such horrifying sport with human life, the heathen heart revealed its kinship with the fallen angels of "Paradise Lost." Nevertheless in that Roman pandemonium there were exceptions—a few hearts of a different cast, in which was at work a silent influence, destined in regal hands to reform the world.

CHAPTER V.

THE INFLUENCE WORKING.

Up in the colonnade reserved for women were two Greek ladies, natives of Asia Minor: Myrtis, a matron of high rank, and her young friend Coryna, a maiden of medium height and of perfect mould, with a wealth of braided auburn hair. The matron wore a *stola*, a long tunic girded in broad folds under the breast, and a white *palla*, a wide upper garment, loosely over her shoulders. Her companion had a white robe with a broad purple border, and over it an azure *palla* covered with golden stars. Both ladies had refined feelings and elegant manners. They were in the Colosseum for the first time.

"What dost thou think of all this, my Myrtis?" enquired Coryna, with a marked expression of pain in her sympathetic countenance.

"Think," answered Myrtis, striving to repress her agitation; "in the dexterity of the combatants I had a gruesome interest, but upon the prostrate, dying men I cannot look"; and the stout but comely woman of tender feeling turned her fair head farther away from the ghastly sight below.

"It is horrible," remarked Coryna, casting a furtive glance into the arena.

"I cannot remain," said Myrtis, "but what would Titanus say?" and she glanced down over the intervening galleries to the *podium*, where her illustrious Roman husband sat.

Beside him was Coryna's brother, Tharsos, a distinguished young officer, wearing a *toga*, with a white *lacerna* or mantle of elegant form.

Behind Titanus stood his young son, Carnion, a raven-haired boy of twelve, dressed in the *toga praetexta*, a becoming garment of white with a wide edge of purple, and suspended from his neck the *bulla*, a round ornament of gold, worn especially by the children of the noble. He held in his hand a cluster of lilies, a little gift meant for Coryna, but which he had forgotten to hand over when entering the amphitheatre.

"See how Carnion is disturbed!" observed Coryna; "the dear boy turns away his head and will not look at the expiring horseman right underneath."

The mother saw her child's attitude with pleased eyes, indeed they were often on him.

"Though tender-hearted, yet my Carnion is brave and strong," said she with a smile of pride.

"He is a soldier, every bit of him," added Coryna. "How different from his elder brother, Dinarchus!"

"Yes, my Dinarchus is a great reader, a young philosopher, a hermit, dear boy. He is now deep in the study of the Christian books. I would my Carnion were at home with him to-day, but he expected to see a wild-beast fight."

"Observe thy husband and my brother—see how calmly they look on!"

"They are soldiers, Coryna, and accustomed as we know to the spectacle of wounds and blood. To them, the arena must be as nothing to a field of battle when the clash of sword and spear is past."

"Oh, it must be racking, revolting!" exclaimed the other, pained at the mental vision of mangled heaps of slain; "and our beloved ones hate the sight."

"They also dislike what they see before them," said Myrtis. "They love skill, but they have no love for wanton play with human life."

"I wish all Rome hated such idle butchery," remarked Coryna earnestly, but rather loudly.

Overhearing these remarks, spoken in the Latin tongue, a number of ladies sneered and smiled. All, or nearly all, who made that wide investing terrace a wreath of brightness and beauty, were dead to pity. At the most they could only feel regret for a wounded favorite or a dying hero.

"I would all the empire were of thy mind, Coryna, and then no such sad spectacle would stain our own beloved, humaner land.

"Christianity is the deadly enemy of all this wicked work. May it prosper!" said the young lady fervently.

"There are no Christians here, I venture to say, civil or military," responded Myrtis. "No follower of the humane Jesus would come within these walls, unless wronged and led, or bent on some heroic deed. But we worshippers of a hundred gods can thank our divinities for no good influence. I hate the gods: may they forgive me!" and the reflective lady smiled at her own bold scepticism.

"They are myths, so my brother says," added Coryna, with a look of decision and relief.

"Tharsos is almost a Christian," remarked Myrtis, "and with him I strongly sympathize."

"He is. But see, he is telling thy husband something, and look how earnestly Carnion watches his words. Of a surety something strange or startling is going to present itself next. The uncertainty about the time of the Christian's appearance must be removed, but my brother's signal will tell."

CHAPTER VI.

THE INDIGNATION OF THARSOS.

Tharsos was speaking with deep but suppressed feeling.

"I have heard of the maiden," he continued, "and have seen her in my native province. Her good deeds to the poor and the suffering have been countless. Her whole life has been work and pity and self-sacrifice. It represents the highest moral beauty."

"Strange," remarked Titanus sympathetically, "that the maiden has held up under prison life so long."

"Though meek and modest," replied Tharsos, "she possesses a fortitude that bears incredible strain. I almost believe, indeed I do believe, that her power must come from Him whom they call Jesus of Nazareth."

"Our laws are evil," said Titanus reflectively, "or such a woman would have known no strain but daily duty. But thou art becoming Christian, Tharsos, yet I do not reproach thee—it were good if all men were."

At this stage the riderless steed kicked a pursuing guard on the palm of his uplifted hand, raised in self defence, and the spectators laughed heartily. Carnion's attention was diverted for a little from the serious conversation, and he stepped a few feet away.

"'Evil,' didst thou say! Our heathen system is corrupt and cursed, an only too ready tool of ignorant malice. For no other reason could the enemies of the accomplished maiden lead her into this arena"; and Tharsos writhed under the thought that justified his grave charge.

Titanus was astonished to see a man so loyal and reflective, and hitherto so quiet and self-possessed, now quivering with indignation.

"Be tranquil, my friend, thou canst not mend matters, and thou hast done thy duty. Hast thou not told me of thy hastening to the Praefect to plead for postponement or release, and that this dignitary had already gone to the Colosseum, with all of the lesser magistrates who had any possible power?"

"I would that I had received the tidings earlier," was the answer, spoken in a low tone of deep sadness, even despair.

"Content thee, my dear Tharsos, thou hast done thy best; and strive to think that speedy death, even if cruel and revolting, is better than prolonged prison-hardship and degradation."

Tharsos turned and looked up at the serried mass of living faces behind him, his indignation now controlled, yet he saw no one—none but the beautiful face of his affectionate sister whom he warmly loved; and there flashed into his heart—"What if she were the victim!" His colour changed and his lips tightened. Some strange thought seemed to enter him, and he arose from his seat.

"Thou wilt, of course, wait and see the maiden?" said Titanus with a perplexed inquiring look.

But Tharsos stood up to his full height, and cast one withering look towards Titanus, as much as if to say—"What, witness the butchery of one like my own sister!" Turning haughtily on his heel, he strode two steps back to the staircase, muttering something in which there was the distinct word Lion, and in a moment he was down and out of view.

CHAPTER VII.

THE PERPLEXITY OF CARNION.

Amidst the laughter and the babel of voices, Carnion's quick ear caught the magic word—Lion!

Turning round into his former place, "Is there a lion coming at last, my father?" he asked eagerly, while his dark eyes sparkled with emotion.

"Yes, my son."

"I am very sorry that Tharsos has gone," remarked the boy, looking at the vomitory (opening) of the staircase.

"He had, he was—rather, he preferred to go; perhaps it is better," said Titanus with a troubled absent look.

"What kind of lion is coming father?" enquired Carnion, his chief interest being in that direction.

"A great lion from Libya, my son, a beast fierce and hungry."

"And with what beasts is it going to fight? Will they be wild-boars, or bears, or tigers, or elephants? How I should love to see a big battle among them all! Tell me, father, what are the beasts to be." And the beautiful boy fairly shook with excitement.

The father did not speak for a moment. His brows lowered over large brown eyes, a crimson wave of shame and anger swept over his handsome face, followed by a subduing wave of pity, and then he spoke in a tone that surprised the ardent boy.

"Carnion," said he, "there is little likelihood that the lion will have anything to fight with."

"Why not, father?" asked the boy, feeling quite disappointed. "Will it only go round the arena and roar?"

"Were that all, my son, I should be exceedingly glad."

The boy was perplexed:—"What dost thou mean, father?"

"I mean, my son, that the lion is to find its prey in the form of a defenceless virtuous woman!"

The boy was amazed and his eyes were piercing. "My father," said he tremulously, "is it the lady Tharsos spoke of?"

"Yes, Carnion."

"Oh father, how cruel!" exclaimed the boy in great distress. "Will nobody fight for her and save her?"

"If any man be found bold enough to face the most formidable brute that ever sprang into the arena—that, and that only may save her," answered Titanus. "But the conditions are hard, so hard that I may say the case is well-nigh hopeless, and the man that would undertake it would either be a fool, impelled by inordinate greed, or filled with god-like self-sacrifice. Neither shield, nor spear, nor sword—nothing but a bronze dagger is to be allowed her defender, should one come forward, and he is to be naked but for a slight girdle around his loins."

"Is there no man compelled to fight, oh father?"

"No one, my son. The defence is voluntary. Both Demonicus and Telassar volunteered; the former is dead, and I fear the latter will back out. Who else would venture, I know not."

"Father," said the boy, in a trembling tone, yet with a ring of purpose in it, "wilt thou permit my absence for a little time?"

"Certainly, my son: it was in my mouth to bid thee look into the street for a little time; or if thy desire be to speak a word with mother thou mayest, but tell my name to the *designator* (seat-attendant). 'Titanus' is enough."

Carnion disappeared.

CHAPTER VIII.

WAITING FOR THE VICTIM.

On the departure of Tharsos, Myrtis had turned and said—

"Thy brother's signal, as thou hast told me, Coryna. Come! let us go."

"It is, but—not yet, dear Myrtis," was the answer in a voice of gentle firmness.

"And in the face of thy brother's strong desire thou art waiting to witness the foul torture and death of a lady refined and good—our fellow-countrywoman too!"

"I shall not behold that," replied the maiden with earnest, hopeful light in her dark hazel eyes: "some brave man will appear; but if not, then I shall turn my back or fly when"—She dared not finish, and Myrtis added—

"When the lion springs. Oh! my Coryna, let us go. This is the work of demons."

"I cannot, Myrtis, I cannot. I shall know the end sooner here."

"There can be but one end, my dear. The cruel crafty managers, bribed to get rid of the maiden without more delay, as Tharsos informed thee, planned this well. What man with a mere dagger could slay a lion? A naked man too. Coryna, the whole work is contemptible, contemptible!" And the deep blue eyes of Myrtis flashed forth her scorn, as she looked down into the arena and scanned it swiftly round till her attention rested anxiously at the eastern end.

"The Romans love effect," Coryna answered bitterly, as she unconsciously twisted her long gold necklace around her thumb,—"The solitary fight will be a striking contrast to the battle that has been."

"There will be no fight, my dear. Who would take such a risk for a woman, a Christian too? But I shall wait with thee, Coryna, and get a glimpse of the poor maiden, and let us hope that her God will help her."

Coryna did not speak, but her expressive face told her gratitude and hope.

The conversation was stopped by the loud blast of trumpets, indicating that another awful act was to begin; and the great hum of voices ceased. The sand was clear of everything, as if a bare, vast, oval table, and all faces were turned toward the eastern extremity of the arena, morbidly hungering for more scenes of skill and blood.

CHAPTER IX.

IN THE ARENA.

Pathema was taken from prison, where she had been shut up for a long time; and the officer in charge was about to open a small door into the arena to lead her in, when a dark-haired boy, the son of illustrious parents, came forward with tears streaming down his noble face, and presented her with a cluster of white lilies. Accepting the flowers speechlessly but gracefully, the doomed maiden bent down with a full heart and kissed him. The lilies reminded her of Him who was made perfect through suffering, and they gave her renewed strength.

"Thy name, my darling?"

"Carnion," was the answer, broken and low.

Stooping down, Pathema put a gentle trembling arm around the boy and kissing him again, she said—

"My lovely one, God bless thee!"

The guard in uniform opened the door and led the innocent victim into the great arena.

"The maiden comes: see, yonder," said Coryna, looking intently towards her.

Myrtis spoke not, but strained her eyes to see.

The Christian maiden approached slowly in charge of the guard till she was placed in front of the pavilion where sat the emperor, clothed in a purple robe and on his head a laurel crown. Leaving her there, the guard withdrew without delay that the keeper might unbar a heavy iron gate for the wild beast to enter in and devour.

Pathema stood alone, a graceful form in flowing garments, within those spacious walls. Clothed in mockery in the white robe of a vestal virgin, yet she was a chaste virgin of Jesus Christ. Bound with a white fillet, her rich black hair, of lavish length, lay back in glistening waves. Her soft dark eyes were modestly towards the ground; once only were they raised, and then to a purer region than earth. Her face was pale and worn but eminently beautiful, with the light of heaven on her thoughtful brow. All around, thousands upon thousands of human eyes, gazing with inhumane curiosity, were an abashing and disturbing sight themselves. But with the solitary object of their gaze, the flow of mental energy was smoothly but strongly and consumingly in the channel of the spiritual emotions. The hidden struggle with conflicting streams of feeling was all gone through in the bitterness and supplications of the dungeon. The agony was past, and Pathema was resigned.

"That sad sweet countenance entrances me," said Myrtis, deeply moved. "Oh Coryna, I go, and yet I cannot! Whence that light and peace?"

Coryna replied not, for she could not. But from among the *pullati* or poor people, immediately below, an answer of a kind came. It was in the subdued voice of a shepherd from the mountains of Lycia. Orestes had nimbly escaped while Pathema was being removed from the prison not long before; but at the risk of recapture he had entered the amphitheatre, determined, like Peter, to see the end, not out of curiosity but of Christian love, hoping against hope. He sat at the end of a seat near one of the *vomitoria* or doors of entrance from the internal lobbies in the shell of the building. Although his garb was soiled and worn, his face was thoughtful, humane and resolute, like the rugged rocks of Taurus. His remarks were not intended for other ears, but were the half-audible, broken sentences of an intense mind.

"Listen!" said Coryna, recovering herself, "he speaks in our own tongue; and they heard such expressions as—

"The peace of God, which passeth all understanding. Enduring—enduring! Life is but a fleeting breath at best. Corrupt—corrupt! Is not this foul spectacle around her the proof? She would not live for a human name—worthless from the low-viewed multitude—nor for pleasure, nor for mere living, at the price of loyalty to Christ. Yet she would live—live that she might humbly aid these people to rise up from the pit of the sensual savage mind—into the light, the glorious light. But she is rejected and despised. Like her Master, she must be sacrificed—in cruelty and shame. If it be possible, let this cup pass from her, I beseech Thee, O God!"

Pathema knew not that in the vast multitude above there was one—her fellow-countryman and co-worker, the humble shepherd of mount Taurus—pleading for her life with all the intensity of agonising pity. To her, mercy was a stranger within those living walls, yet with meekly bended head in steadfast trust she stood, bearing her awful cross in the footprints of the Nazarene.

CHAPTER X.

THE LION.

The great iron gate was opened up. Into the arena proudly leaped a glowing-eyed gigantic brute, with tawny coat and heavy mane, the hungry king of the forest.

All eyes were directed towards him, but Pathema moved not.

"Now may her God help her!" exclaimed Myrtis, bending her head and burying her face in her hands; but unable to bear the strain, she rose up and left, leaving her companion absorbed and pained, and her husband down on the *podium*, transfixed yet ashamed.

No wild-beast fighter having appeared—no one to gratify the craving for excitement—a great hum of disappointment soon ascended and rolled round the amphitheatre.

The lion raised his massive head as if in defiance, and uttered a mighty, vibrant roar.

The hum of voices stopped.

Pathema's heart trembled in the balance, as a topmast twig before the first breath of darkening storm. The mere finite fabric would surely have given way. But if the tremor lasted in varying degree, hesitation had perched for a moment only. Prolonged habit, woven in as metal cord, called forth the virtue told in the oft-read words—"What time I am afraid, I will trust in thee." Strengthened from above, she calmly turned her head and, as if also in defiance, fixed her eyes full upon the distant savage brute.

The hungry lion saw the human form—ah! this was strange choice game. He trod forward with swaying tail—he crept—he crouched low—he would soon spring—and that fair image of the divine would be struck down, torn asunder, bled and crunched in pieces!

Was there no eye to pity, none to save?

"Oh that I were a soldier, a gladiator,—no, just a man, a man!" said Coryna from the depth of a throbbing heart, "then would I rush to the rescue and save her or die!"

The shepherd could not stand the sight, and as he rose to go away his face was ghastly white. As he turned with vacant eyes to walk up the *scalaria* or steps to the door in the *balteus* or wall behind, a voice at his elbow said in the Greek language—

"Here! take this true dagger, friend."

"Why?" replied the shepherd, looking bewildered.

"Dost thou not know the terms?" answered the Greek.

"I am a stranger. What terms?" Orestes asked eagerly.

"Oh, I thought thou hadst resolved to go to the woman's aid," replied the man, disappointed.

"Give me the dagger," said the shepherd, a red flush rushing into his cheek. He had now grasped the situation at a glance, and seizing the weapon without ceremony or further word, he sprang up three or four steps and passed through the vomitory of the wall to the stairs leading down to the lower part of the building.

Coryna heard and saw with joy, but with the racking pain of suspense, for the shepherd might be—(she dared not think it) would likely be—too late!

There was a brief, awful lull.

The lion would not leap while those calm heavenly eyes shone full upon him, and he would not as long as they retained strength. But if Pathema's head would bow down or turn aside, or if her vital force would go, and it could not last long, there would then be the sure and fatal spring.

During this critical pause, Carnion returned. He gave a half-expectant, eager glance down into the arena. Had there been a mere wild-beast battle—had the lion been face to face with an Indian tiger, the sight to the boy would naturally have been grand; but now it was perplexing and sore. He saw his thread-like hope of rescue broken—the monster glared upon a frail beautiful woman, and, as yet, there was no man. Turning aside, he bent his head on the back of the young officer's empty chair, and hid his tearful eyes, saying to himself despairingly—

"Will no brave man come, before it is too late?"

CHAPTER XI.

THE MAN WITH THE DAGGER.

Another door opened up with a sudden bang, and behold! a fair-haired youth, almost naked, and armed with a simple dagger, stepped boldly into the arena. A great shout went up from the spectators, as, without the least delay, he ran forward and stood between the lion and its intended victim.

Coryna gave the would-be deliverer one bewildered, piercing glance, then instantly lowering her head she hid a face of death-like whiteness in hands clammy with a cold perspiration.

"Father, father, dost thou not know him?" cried Carnion, startled up with the bang and the shout, and quivering with mingled grief and joy.

Titanus, never without a feeble ray of hope, was yet thunderstruck when the combatant's identity dawned upon him; and though filled with admiration, he was visibly troubled.

The brave youth below stood erect and resolute, while the beast, disconcerted with the shout and the sudden check, rested back flat upon its limbs and belly. Like David of old when facing the giant, the young man came forward trusting in the God of Israel.

"Who is that courageous but foolhardy venturer?" enquired the emperor.

"Tharsos, of the praetorian guard, O sovereign."

"One of my noblest and wealthiest officers!" exclaimed the emperor; "yet let him go—he tends towards the detested Christians," added he haughtily.

Servilius, the pagan confidant of the emperor, but the enemy of Tharsos, was secretly delighted. "We shall soon get rid of him, and Emerentia will be mine," said he to himself, as he leaned over to take a satisfied, last look at the self-sacrificing nobleman below.

Pathema was struck with amazement, but inexpressibly grieved to think that the fair form of her defender would be speedily felled to the earth, and mangled, and devoured!

Tharsos did not stand on the defensive: he took the first step to battle; and the people gave a deafening shout of approval. He moved towards the formidable lion with slow but firm tread. The mysterious light of the steadfast human eye was unbearable—the suspicious beast rose up and skulked away, with trailing tail and with head turned partly round to keep watch upon its enemy. Tharsos held on steadily, purposing that if death should happen to him, it would be as far away as possible from the eyes of the sore-tried, desolate maiden.

When near the side of the arena right opposite the emperor, the lion howled with fear and sprang ten feet up towards the balcony, its eye-balls gleaming just a short space below Titanus and his eager boy.

Rising up quickly, Titanus placed his hand upon the hilt of his sword. Fain would he have leapt down to the aid of his beloved friend. Their eyes met for a moment; and, though pale and grave, Tharsos smiled.

Baffled in its leap, the brute turned sharply round, face to face with its determined pursuer, and uttered a terrific roar of rage. The issue would soon be decided, and the immense concourse of people held their breath, while Pathema turned away her head and offered up a silent prayer to Him who has power over the beast of the field.

Tharsos now drew slowly back, while keeping his eyes towards the enraged lion. Suddenly withdrawing his gaze, he turned and ran with swift and bounding steps straight for the eastern extremity of the arena, while the surprised spectators yelled their contempt after him. Then the man strangely swayed and tottered in front of the very door where the calm resolute woman had entered but a few minutes before.

"He plays the coward, he faints, curse him!" was heard on every hand, as they saw him finally throw up his arms and fall.

"The charge is false, false!" exclaimed an erect, indignant figure with a pale face up among the women. It was the voice of Coryna, but amidst the clamour she was not heard except by those immediately around her.

"Hear ye the madwoman!" cried they, as they scoffed and laughed.

The emperor, disappointed and even ashamed, sat in scornful silence. But Servilius, excited with malignant pleasure, laughed outright.

Then Titanus rose up and drew his glitter-sword. He stepped to the very edge of the balcony, Carnion at his side, and the eyes of the people catching sight of him, the loud storm of abuse instantly ceased.

"Too late, too late, and out of order!" Servilius fiercely cried, fearing the rescue of the man he unjustly hated.

"He who calls my friend Tharsos a coward!" exclaimed Titanus in clear ringing voice, "shall die. I challenge him to meet me next on the sand of that arena!"

And Coryna was unspeakably relieved.

But no man would wantonly accept the challenge, for Titanus was agile and strong, and was one of the most expert swordsmen in the Roman army.

There was, however, much excitement over this bold interruption and at the announcement of the name of the prostrate man, whose high rank was widely known.

The indignant Titanus was right—there was no cowardice. The multitude had entirely misjudged the tactics of the brave Tharsos. The fallen man lay quietly upon his back, with his face slightly toward the lion, and with his dagger closely clinched in his strong right hand.

Coryna's feelings were strung to the highest pitch. Her suspense was agony, but she would not have her brave brother elsewhere.

The ferocious beast, taken by surprise or freed from provocation, suddenly quieted down. It sat on its haunches for a moment, and looked after the fleeing man. Then it rose up, and preferring a fallen form to an erect, it followed him with light majestic tread. It came to within twenty feet of where he lay, and halted, sitting on its haunches again. Rising up, it walked around him twice, looking at him curiously all the time. Satisfied at last that it had an easy prey, it went forward softly, like a cat. Halting, it bent down to sniff the still, white, helpless-like figure, and to seize the flank.

The time for action had come. Swiftly Tharsos drew his arm, and with terrific force thrust the dagger right into the would-be devourer's heart!

With a mighty yell the lion leaped into the air, and fell heavily across the body of its destroyer—a dangerous struggle or two, and it was dead!

Then was the stratagem understood, and when it was coupled with the name and rank of the self-sacrificing victor, a thundering shout of applause filled the amphitheatre.

"Well done! brave Tharsos," said the Emperor proudly to the distinguished noblemen around him, who were all delighted, Servilius excepted, who vainly strove to conceal his deep displeasure.

Looking deliberately across the arena, the emperor caught Titanus' eye and smiled. That valiant officer rose up and saluted his sovereign with becoming dignity and grace.

"Oh father, what a grand fight," exclaimed Carnion, "and the Christian lady is free!"

"Yes, my son," replied the trustful soldier, resting back upon the chair for a moment with unutterable satisfaction, for the honor of his friend was upheld, and the virtuous maiden was saved.

The vast multitude were greatly gratified in their feeling of the sensational. Yet a few were stirred to better thoughts and high resolves, who would never otherwise be influenced. Thus in the providence of God does the wrath of man work out His purpose and praise.

The applause was at its height. But, strange to say, Tharsos moved not. The officials that had gone to his aid removed the huge dead lion from his body. Still Tharsos moved not. Something appeared to be wrong, and the great noise stopped. The spectators leaned forward and looked anxious. Was the dauntless destroyer himself destroyed? The attendants turned him tenderly over—when, alas! there was a frightful gash in his naked side, from which the blood was flowing freely into the sand. His face and lips were white, with an expression of peace, as if in death.

Titanus, deeply anxious, arose and hastened away to get the best physician he could find. As he disappeared he glanced upward to the colonnade, but Coryna, the sister, was gone.

Carnion remained to see more of the stricken man, and of the pale woman in the centre, silent, unnoticed, and alone.

Promptly but gently the attendants lifted up Tharsos and carried him from the arena. And as he passed from their sight the vast audience was hushed in regret.

CHAPTER XII.

DISCIPLINE.

Pathema also watched their movements and departure, fearing that the wounded youth was dead. Her heart yearned anxiously after him. Who was he that had so valiantly fought and bled for her? His name was Tharsos, and he was a brave, self-sacrificing nobleman—that was all she could tell. It was enough. Self-sacrifice vividly recalled another sacrifice, greater, perfect, and for all. The flood-gate of feeling could not be kept closed. She held the lilies in her drooping hand, she raised them, looked at them tenderly for a moment, then buried her face in them, and wept.

A herald now approached Pathema and formally announced that she was free, at the same time pointing to the open door through which they had borne the bleeding hero. But to the sensual undiscerning multitude, Pathema was no heroine. She was only a woman; and in those days when heathenism prevailed, women were not honoured as they are now. Besides, Pathema was to them a fanatic, a detested Christian, and at best but a stubborn, unbending, young woman. They knew not her supreme gentleness and modesty, which shrank from publicity like a sensitive plant from touch. They did not know that it was intense love and loyalty to her Head which gave her strength to dare even cruel death.

Pathema turned to leave the arena, but the tension and turmoil and reaction were now telling fast upon her fragile frame. As she walked away, her weakness was so great that she had the utmost difficulty to keep from falling, and it was only too visible; but she struggled on.

There was no sign of sympathy from the now talkative crowd, wailing for another scene of blood. They treated her with indifference—she was but a very secondary actor in the tragedy. Yet, though they knew her not, she was the greater victor, not that day alone, but in her past daily life of sacrifice. She was greater than he that slays a lion or takes a city!

Among the indifferent crowd there was one bright exception. Carnion, though not then a Christian, yet was fulfilling the beautiful words—"Rejoice with them that do rejoice, and weep with them that weep." As Pathema walked away with bowed head and faltering steps, the lad stepped to the edge of the balcony, and waiving his silken handkerchief, called out—"Thy God bless thee!" And the sufferer heard the boy's sweet, strengthening voice, and struggled on.

Misunderstood and unregarded by the heartless multitude, yet Pathema's discipline and victory were the work of God, and they, even the greatest of them, were but the willing, guilty instruments. She was being fashioned through suffering in the truest beauty and for the highest honour—the beauty of holiness, which endures for ever. She walked meekly and painfully on, she reached the little door, and then she passed from their guilty presence,—a queen, though uncrowned.

CHAPTER XIII.

NIGHT.

The unconscious officer's wound was hastily but skilfully bound up and the blood stanched, he was raised in a *lectica* or litter, and carried home with great care to his mansion. In the quietest chamber of the house, he was laid upon a costly bed, one of rare wood with feet of ivory and with purple coverlets curiously broidered with gold.

Titanus, having done his utmost, had gone away with Carnion, much cast down, the more so that he was under command by the emperor to leave Rome immediately on foreign service.

Coryna was left beside her brother, with the physician and a faithful intelligent slave. The depth of her feelings could not be sounded, yet there was staying power of a kind. Grief, admiration and anxiety surged around a will of rock. Within, a whirling storm: without, a pallid calm. She watched for the first signs of consciousness as the eagle watches for its prey.

Tharsos lay as if in death, with the soft light of serenity still on his manly face and classic brow. He moved at last and opened his eyes.

"Where is the Christian maiden?" said he in dreamy feebleness, his expression changing into a look of anxiety.

Much relieved in tension, Coryna answered softly—

"Some kind one quickly conveyed her away, my brother, but I have sent several of our slaves over the city to find out her lodging-place and to enquire after her health."

A radiant joy covered his face, and he remained silent for a little. Then he spoke with quiet earnestness:—

"My sister, thou knowest her worth. Look after her, I pray thee, for her own sake, and for the sake of Him she serves so well. But"—and here he halted, trying painfully to take a deep breath.

"Speak not, my brother," said Coryna soothingly.

Becoming calm, he resumed—"Hasten the search, Coryna; ask the maiden to come and see me before I die. Tell her that I shall regard her visit as a kindness and honour. I desire much to speak to her, my beloved sister, to place thee in her care, and then I shall die in peace." Tharsos spoke these last words very feebly, and then closing his eyes he sank bask into unconsciousness.

Coryna's heart was torn, but she would not renounce hope.

It was difficult to trace where Pathema had gone, humble Christian friends having taken her to a remote, obscure, but comfortable home. One messenger, however, got word of her whereabouts late the same night, but too late to be prudent to call. When he knocked at the door next day he did not know that the object of his search was well informed through her friends concerning Tharsos' critical state, and that already there was a brief, beautiful, tablet-letter in her own handwriting, lying near his unconscious pillow.

Weakened by her cruel experience, Pathema was resting quietly upon a couch beside a small open window, her heart full of gratitude to God for deliverance and of anxiety about her human deliverer.

"Is there a maiden named Pathema lodging here?" Marcellus, the messenger, enquired.

"There is, sir," said a little Roman maid, the daughter of the hostess, much excited as she looked out into the street and saw six slaves in red livery standing beside a grand palanquin.

"My master, Tharsos, is at the point of death, but he would like to see the Christian maiden ere he die."

Pathema overheard these words, and rose up at once. Though weak in body, she was resolute in mind, and she had enjoyed a providential night's rest. There was no delay in arranging matters, and she stepped into the *lectica* calmly but as one about to go through a painful ordeal.

After elbowing their way through the streets, Marcellus leading, the slaves at length laid their burden down beside a statue of Caractacus in the vestibule before the door of the young nobleman's mansion.

Like the usual Roman dwelling, the exterior was not prepossessing; but when Marcellus opened the door, the prospective view was peculiarly magnificent. The doors and curtains of successive courts were drawn aside, revealing active fountains, marble pillars with splendid statuary, and a lawn and shrubbery exposed above to the blue Italian sky.

Pathema ascended the marble steps, and passing through the richly gilded door inlaid with tortoise-shell, she stood for a moment on the mosaic floor of the *ostium* or entrance hall. Overhead, a parrot of brilliant plumage greeted her with the salutation, "Joy be with thee." Going straight on for a few feet, she passed into the *atrium*, a pillared court, where Coryna, the image of Tharsos in finer mould, met her and kissed her hand in touching silence.

Leading the way, Coryna went on through the *cavaedium*, a larger Corinthian-columned court, in whose centre stood a splashing fountain, shooting its crystal stream towards the open sky. Passing the *tablinum* or room of archives, they proceeded into the *peristylium*, a still larger transverse court or lawn with verdant shrubbery and a chaste towering fountain.

Here there was a Roman lady, elegantly dressed and richly jewelled. Her dark-complexioned face was strikingly beautiful, yet marred by a lofty look of haughtiness. She walked around the lawn with the alert graceful movements of a panther. Evidently she was laboring under considerable excitement, and when Coryna and Pathema entered, her black eyes flashed out a deadly scorn.

Inwardly disturbed, yet meeting the lady's look with a smile, Coryna turned aside between the marble columns into one of the *exedrae* or rooms for conversation. Guiding Pathema to a comfortable seat, she spoke for the first time, saying,

"Welcome to our home!"

"I thank thee for the honour," answered Pathema, "and I am glad to come, yet greatly pained."

"My brother did right," was the quiet response.

"Receive, I pray thee," said Pathema in tears, "my deepest gratitude for thy brother's deed."

"Tharsos will yet receive it personally," was the happy answer.

"I rejoice to hear thy hope," replied Pathema with brightening eyes.

"I have hope, but the physicians have little or none."

After a little further conversation during which the visitor's whole heart was drawn out to the noble character before her, Coryna craved liberty for a moment to bid her friend in the *peristylium* farewell. As she went out, a female slave entered to wait upon Pathema and show her every necessary attention. The slave was not long in her presence when she bewailed the calamity that had come upon her beloved master. Then she mentioned that the young lady in the *peristylium* was much distressed.

"Emerentia," she continued, "loves him exceedingly, and he liked her in return. Her father and mother leave to-day for a distant city of the empire, and she goes with them."

Pathema was grieved, and she expressed the fervent hope that the nobleman would recover, for the distressed lady's sake, as well as his own.

"Emerentia," added the slave, "is generous and accomplished—that is why the master liked her—but her goodness is not so strong as her pride and jealousy. The lady is fierce in her feelings. She hates the Christians, and more so now than ever."

After a few minutes Coryna returned, restrained and quiet, but with the trace of a tear that had stolen down her fair face.

"My brother," said she with hesitation, "earnestly desired that thou shouldst come and stay with me for a time. Is this possible? May I hope it is."

Pathema was taken by surprise. Her home and beloved parents and the poor of Patara had been much in her heart. Her father had been more than once in Rome, trying to obtain her liberty, and he had provided long ago the temporary abode she had been carried to by Christian friends. This now swept across her vision. But it was quickly followed by another picture—the self-sacrificing act of the nobleman in whose mansion she was now a guest. And he was dying—so the physicians feared. Duty—gratitude—consolation—everything demanded her presence. Her answer was unhesitating and prompt—

"I will stay with thee."

And Coryna bent down and kissed her, with a feeling that was warmly returned.

Tharsos was beyond the stage of knowing anyone. In spite of the best medical skill, fever had quickly set in, and the battle began in earnest between life and death.

Now was the opportunity for a woman's soldiership—soldiership of the highest kind—where woman only can excel. The weapons are experience, presence of mind, patience, endurance and compassion. With all these Pathema was perfectly armed, her value was speedily recognised, and she became an unassuming soldier in the strife. There were days and nights of anxious care and watching, the utmost was performed, and nothing left undone. Yet Tharsos seemed to be marching straight without resource to the grim enemy's gloomy gate. The thought was painful beyond measure, but it seemed to Pathema that the noble-minded man must die!

While the fever lay upon him he spoke in bits of sentences about the Nazarene, mysterious, divine! and the devoted disciple Pathema. His language was now subdued and reverential, tender and touching, as if he stood in the presence of unearthly beings; then indignant, emphatic, even wild, as if he were again surrounded by the cruel and inquisitive multitude—a wildness wholly unlike that of the quiet reserved man in health. Sitting up and pointing to the walls he would cry—

"Great God! the fiends, mad, malignant, blood-thirsty, the fiends of Tartarus have entered thy fair world in the bodies of men."

CHAPTER XIV.

DAY.

Tharsos did not die. Had the lion's claws twisted, or torn a little deeper, or had there been incapable nursing, there would have been no hope. But the animal missed the vitals, and the faithful nurse made the most of what remained—she would have readily yielded life at her loving though painful duty.

When the consuming fever was completely turned and past, and a little strength gained through death-like sleep and judicious nourishment, it dawned upon the sick man's mind that someone strange but fascinating was constantly by his side. And when he learned that his attendant was Pathema, there came a peace over his soul that could not be expressed.

After a long time Tharsos recovered strength, but he was never again the same. He was subject to spells of weakness that kept him to his couch for days, and he had to resign his position in the army. Yet he lived for many years afterwards, and did a noble work, impossible to be done in the service of the emperor, a work that could not be hid, as a good soldier of Jesus Christ.

Pathema, relieved in due time, went back to her home in Asia Minor. She carried many costly gifts, showered upon her and refused in vain. But, better still, she carried away the undying devotion of Tharsos, the close sisterly affection of Coryna, and the goodwill of all that really knew her worth.

Her parents in Patara were overjoyed at her return, and so were many others in the city and wide surroundings—many, who waited for tender attention and waited not in vain.

Tharsos sold his mansion in Rome, and followed Pathema to Patara. He bought a beautiful residence in that city, and built another farther up the river Xanthus among the hills. And Pathema became his wife. Staying in these two houses alternately, at different seasons of the year, they passed the rest of their lives. No two beings loved ouch other better, or did a more useful and beneficent work. Their city home was a centre of Christian light and hospitality, while their rural retreat was the scene of many joyous and instructive gatherings of the country people. In these abodes the friendless wanderer, of whatever race or tribe, could lay down his weary head and there find solace and rest.

CHAPTER XV.

SAINT NICHOLAS.

"The house among the olive trees at the base of yonder hill—whose is it, friend?" enquired a traveller of a pagan whom he met.

"The hospitable home of Tharsos and Pathema," was the reply.

"Thanks be to God!" said the traveller, passing on.

"Who are these two men that sit together in the portico?" asked he of a Christian as he came up in front of the house.

"Tharsos, the owner of the mansion, and Orestes, a shepherd from the valley beyond."

"They speak as brothers," said the traveller, raising his eyebrows and passing by.

Going to a side door, he was about to knock when a woman approached from behind luxuriant vines, with a twig of olive blossoms in her hand. She walked towards him with quiet grace, her countenance inspiring all respect and trust.

Bowing low, the traveller said—"My name is Timon. I have travelled far, and am footsore and in want."

"Enter in," said Pathema kindly, "sit at yonder table with the rest, and thou shalt have water to wash thy feet."

Going in, the ex-detective was met by a pretty boy with golden hair and deep blue eyes, the first-born son of Tharsos and Pathema. The child took a gentle hold of his sun-brown hand to lead him to food and rest. The weary stranger clasped the tender fingers, and looking down into the trusting, thoughtful face, he said—-

"Child of a noble mother, thou hast made me glad."

"Come," said the little one lovingly, "come."

"Tell me thy name, darling."

"My name is Nicholas," replied the boy.

"Thou art a little saint," rejoined the stranger hopefully, "and thou shalt gladden many."

Wonderful boy of long ago!
Come now and tell—

As aged man, with beard of snow
And hair all white, what gave thy name,
Adown the years, the glow of fame?
Explain thy spell

O'er countless children waiting thee
In varied home,—
Afar inland, beside the sea,
In lonely cot, and crowded town,—
Awatching oft in midnight gown,
For thee to come.

Wert thou a selfish, cunning boy?
Ah no, ah no!
Tradition findeth no alloy
In thy make-up, but giveth thee
A generous heart, from baseness free,
Alike the snow.

White out and in, a giver pure,
With heart all warm,—
This! is thy spell, direct and sure,
O'er boy and girl; who think it good
To paint thy face in comic mood—
It does no harm.

But clothed in loving, reverent mien
Tradition gives—
Thou art, in this, by seniors seen,
To meet the life of one who was
The mother of Saint Nicholas:
In thee she lives.